IMAGINE THAT

Licensed exclusively to Imagine That Publishing Ltd
Tide Mill Way, Woodbridge, Suffolk, IP12 1AP, UK
www.imaginethat.com
Copyright © 2019 Imagine That Group Ltd
All rights reserved
0 2 4 6 8 9 7 5 3 1
Manufactured in China

Written by Joshua George
Illustrated by Barbara Bakos

ISBN 978-1-78700-893-9

A catalogue record for this book is available from the British Library

For Camilla, who is always very well behaved.

NO MORE MONKEYS!

Written by Joshua George

Illustrated by Barbara Bakos

Alfie lived at home with his mum,
his dad, his sister ...

... and a troop of monkeys. For some reason, no one could see the monkeys except Alfie. That was just the way it was.

The monkeys were great fun, and they were always ready to play with Alfie. They loved climbing and running around the garden making loud monkey noises.

But they were a little bit naughty.

One day, Alfie and the monkeys had fun digging an enormous hole in the garden.

When Alfie came inside he washed his hands,
but the monkeys didn't wash theirs,
and soon there was dirt everywhere!

'Oh, Alfie,' moaned Mum,
'what a mess you've made!'

'But it wasn't me, it was
the monkeys,' said Alfie.

'No more monkeys,'
said Mum. 'OK?'

'OK,' said Alfie.

The next day, Alfie was quietly doing some colouring when the monkeys grabbed his crayons and started decorating the walls.

'Aaaarrrgggghhh!' yelled Mum.
'What have you done, Alfie?'

'But it wasn't me, it was the monkeys,' said Alfie.

'No more monkeys,' said Mum. 'OK?'

'OK,' said Alfie. 'I'll tell them to stop being so naughty.'

Upstairs in Alfie's bedroom, the monkeys were swinging from the curtains and bouncing on the bunk bed.

And when Alfie tried to tell them to stop being so naughty, they were having too much fun to listen!

The next evening, Alfie and his sister had chocolate ice cream after dinner.

Suddenly, one of the monkeys popped up from under the table, took a scoop of Alfie's ice cream, and then smeared it all over Alfie's face.

'Mum!' whined Alfie's sister.
'Look what Alfie's done!'

'Oh, Alfie,' said Mum,
'what have you done now?'

'But it wasn't me, it was
a monkey,' said Alfie.

'No more monkeys,'
said Mum. 'OK?'

'OK,' said Alfie.

For a few days, Alfie hardly saw the monkeys. Perhaps they had stopped making trouble after all.

Then one morning, as he was getting ready for school, the monkeys grabbed Alfie, put his socks on his hands and his shirt on back to front, and then tickled him with their little monkey fingers.

'Oh, Alfie,' sighed Mum.

'It was the monkeys,' laughed Alfie. 'They did it!'

'No more monkeys!' said Mum. 'And that's final.'

'OK,' said Alfie. But he was beginning to wonder if the monkeys would ever stop.

That night, when everyone had gone to bed,
Alfie got up and turned the light on.

'You are too naughty!' he told the monkeys.
'You'll have to go and live somewhere else!
No one wants to live with naughty
little monkeys like you!'

One by one, the monkeys picked up their bags and walked quietly out of the room.

Alfie felt a bit mean, but with no monkeys around he was as good as gold. Mud stayed in the garden, crayons stayed on the paper and Alfie's socks stayed on his feet.

'Are you alright?' asked Mum.

How to be a Good Boy

Later that day, Mum asked Alfie
to help make a chocolate cake.
He whisked the eggs, measured
the flour and got everything
just right. He was a
very good boy!

But when Mum went to answer the phone,
the cake mix looked too good to resist.

Alfie stuck one finger in and had a little taste.

Can you guess what
happened next?

When Mum came back into the room, she saw Alfie and then started laughing so much that she had to sit on the floor!

'Aren't you angry?' asked Alfie.

'Let's get you cleaned up!' laughed Mum.

'Goodnight, you little monkey,'
said Mum as she tucked Alfie
into bed that night. 'I love you!'

'Even if I am a little bit naughty?' asked Alfie.

'Of course!' said Mum.

And that's how Alfie knew the monkeys could come back and live with him.

Even if they were a little bit naughty!